Copyright ©

All rig

The characters and events portrayed in this book are
fictitious. Any similarity to real persons, living or dead,
is coincidental and not intended by the author.

CONTENTS

PREFACE

This book is dedicated to the quiet souls, the introspective hearts, and the wonderfully unique individuals who often find themselves on the sidelines, yearning for connection. To those who've ever felt the sting of social isolation, the awkward silence of an unreturned smile, or the overwhelming anxiety of a crowded room—this one's for you.

It's dedicated to the ones who have spent countless nights staring at screens, wishing for a different reality, a reality where genuine laughter and shared moments are the norm, not the exception. To the dreamers who believe in the power of human connection but haven't yet found the key to unlocking its boundless potential.

This book is a testament to the resilience of the human spirit, the extraordinary capacity for growth, and the possibility of transforming even the most challenging social landscapes. It's a celebration of the quiet strength within, the unwavering potential to blossom, and the courage it takes to step out of the shadows and into the radiant sunshine of fulfilling relationships.

To everyone who has struggled, is struggling, or will struggle with social anxiety—know this: you are not alone. Your unique perspective is a gift, your quiet strength is a superpower, and your journey to connection is worth every step. This book is a guide, a companion, a beacon of hope along your path. It is a testament to the transformative power of self-belief, the magic of genuine connection, and the incredible journey toward a more socially confident and fulfilling you. May it serve as a compass, guiding you toward the warm embrace of friendship, belonging, and the joyous symphony of shared experiences. May it empower you to rewrite your own narrative, to create a life richer with genuine human connection, and to fully embrace the vibrant tapestry of your potential. This dedication is a small token of gratitude for your courage and perseverance, and a promise that better days – and more meaningful connections – lie ahead.

CHAPTER 1: THE LONELY ALGORITHM

The Weight of Silence

The hum of the refrigerator, a low thrumming counterpoint to the rhythmic tap-tap-tap of his keyboard, was the soundtrack to Gary's evenings. His apartment, a meticulously organized space reflecting the precise order he imposed on his life, felt more like a carefully constructed fortress than a home. Minimalist decor, stark lines, and the absence of clutter mirrored his own carefully controlled emotional landscape. He'd always valued solitude, finding comfort in the predictable rhythm of his days, a self-imposed routine that shielded him from the unpredictable chaos of human interaction. But tonight, the quiet was deafening.

The glow of the laptop screen illuminated his face, highlighting the faint lines etching themselves around his eyes—lines carved not by age, but by the persistent ache of loneliness. He scrolled through social media, a curated stream of perfectly filtered lives, each post a vibrant testament to connections he lacked. Laughing faces, celebratory gatherings, intimate moments – a kaleidoscope of experiences that felt both tantalizingly close and impossibly distant. A pang of envy, sharp and familiar, pierced the carefully constructed walls of his composure.

He wasn't actively unhappy, not in the dramatic, tear-soaked sense. His life was, in many ways, successful. He had a stable job as a freelance graphic designer, a comfortable apartment, and enough money to indulge in his hobbies. He enjoyed his work, finding solace in the intricate detail of his designs, the quiet satisfaction of creating something beautiful. His passion for photography often led him to the quiet corners of the city, capturing the subtle beauty in urban landscapes, the stark contrast between concrete and nature. He found a certain peace in the solitude of his hikes, the rhythmic crunch of leaves under his boots a meditative counterpoint to the city's frenetic energy.

But these solitary pursuits, far from filling the void, only seemed to amplify it. The beauty he captured through his lens felt incomplete, lacking the shared experience, the shared appreciation that would have elevated it to something more. The silence of the trails, while initially soothing, often morphed into a crushing weight, the absence of conversation echoing the emptiness within. He'd tried to connect through his hobbies, joining a photography club, attending hiking group meetups. But those attempts had consistently ended in a familiar pattern of awkward silences, forced smiles, and the lingering feeling of being an outsider looking in.

The photography club had been particularly disheartening. He'd carefully selected his best prints, anticipating eager feedback, hoping for a spark of connection. Instead, he'd been met with polite nods, cursory compliments, and the swift diversion of attention elsewhere. The hiking group, though less formal, had been no better. The shared activity failed to bridge the conversational chasm. He'd tried to engage, asking tentative questions about camera settings or hiking trails, only to be met with brief, monosyllabic answers that quickly shut down any possibility of meaningful dialogue. He was left alone in his quiet, and his attempts to make friends had left him with a heavier silence than ever.

His apartment, meticulously clean and organized, was a testament to his controlled existence. Every item had its place, every surface gleamed. Yet it lacked warmth, the inviting chaos of lived experience absent. It wasn't simply the absence of physical objects, but the absence of laughter, of shared meals, of casual conversations that made it feel emotionally barren. The silence in his apartment was a reflection of the silence within him, a silence born not of peace but of isolation. It was a silence he was starting to find unbearable.

Evenings were the worst. He'd meticulously plan his meals, preparing them with precision, but eating alone felt like a ritualistic act of self-imposed punishment. The carefully crafted meals, the perfect lighting, all the small details failed to fill the gaping emptiness left by the lack of human interaction. His evenings were consumed by work, often spilling into the late hours, a form of escape, a way to avoid the stark reality of his loneliness. The endless scrolling through social media only served to intensify his feelings of inadequacy, an endless parade of perfectly posed lives mocking his own quiet existence.

He tried to tell himself that he was perfectly content, that he didn't need the constant noise and drama of social engagement. He'd read articles about the virtues of solitude, the importance of self-reliance, the productivity of introversion. But the carefully constructed arguments fell apart under the weight of his own experience. He knew, deep down, that he craved connection, that the carefully curated silence of his life was a shield, a defense mechanism against a fear he couldn't quite name, a fear that paralyzed him every time he attempted to reach out, to connect. The fear of rejection, the fear of failure, the fear of being seen for who he really was – a man who yearned for connection, yet felt utterly incapable of achieving it.

The unspoken words hung heavy in the air, a silent testament to his missed opportunities, his aborted attempts, his self-imposed isolation. He knew he was intelligent, capable, and creative. But in social situations, these qualities seemed to vanish, replaced by awkward fumbling, stammering words, and a burning sense of inadequacy. He yearned to break free from the weight of silence, to shed the solitary existence that had become both his comfort and his curse. He dreamed of genuine connection, a sense of belonging, a place where he wasn't just a silent observer, but an active participant, a friend, a companion.

His desire for connection simmered beneath the surface, a quiet, persistent longing that shadowed even his most enjoyable moments. He often found himself pausing during his solitary hikes, gazing at groups of people laughing and talking, feeling the sharp sting of exclusion. The sharp contrast between his carefully planned solitude and his deep-seated desire for connection formed a persistent dissonance, a constant tension that left him feeling both drained and agitated. He knew things had to change. He knew this couldn't go on. But the path forward remained shrouded in uncertainty, a daunting unknown stretching before him. He was adrift in a sea of silence, a lonely algorithm in a world desperately searching for a connection that felt just out of reach.

The crisp autumn air nipped at Gary's cheeks as

he walked, the crunch of leaves under his boots a familiar rhythm in his solitary routine. He'd chosen a less frequented path, a narrow track winding through a copse of trees, their leaves ablaze with the fiery hues of fall. The park, usually a sanctuary of quiet contemplation, offered a welcome escape from the relentless hum of the city. He'd always found solace in the solitude of nature, the vastness of the landscape mirroring the expansiveness of his own inner world, a space he usually guarded carefully.

Today, however, the familiar peace felt…different. A subtle unease, a low-level anxiety he couldn't quite place, gnawed at the edges of his calm. He'd been feeling more acutely than usual the weight of his loneliness, the chasm between his carefully constructed life and the longing for genuine connection. The perfectly framed photos he captured on his walks seemed to mock him, exquisite snapshots of a world he couldn't fully inhabit, a world where he remained an outsider looking in.

He rounded a bend in the path, his gaze fixed on the muted colours of the undergrowth, when something caught his eye. Half-hidden beneath a tangle of fallen leaves, a book lay discarded. It was small, its cover worn and faded, the title barely visible. He knelt, brushing away the leaves with a cautious hand, his curiosity piqued. The title, revealed in fragments, read: "The Top Secret Guide to Social Success."

A wry smile touched his lips. "Top Secret," he murmured, a faint echo in the hushed stillness of the park. The irony wasn't lost on him. A "top secret" guide to something as elusive and unpredictable as social success seemed almost absurd. He picked it up, turning it over in his hands. The cover was a dull, almost greyish-brown, the paper creased and softened by time and weather. It felt surprisingly heavy for its size, as if holding more than just words within its pages.

His initial impulse was to leave it. To leave it where it had lain, undisturbed, unseen. It felt almost like an intrusion, this promise of a solution to a problem he hadn't quite admitted to himself. He preferred his carefully crafted solitude, his predictable routine. The idea of actively pursuing social success felt almost…daunting, an overwhelming task he wasn't sure he was equipped to undertake. He was comfortable in his isolation, in the familiar silence of his own company.

But something in the book's worn cover, its mysteriously bold title, whispered a different message, a subtle invitation to explore the uncharted territories of his own heart. He felt a strange pull, a sense of almost hesitant hope, a flicker of something he hadn't felt in a long time – curiosity. The book, abandoned and forgotten by its previous owner, seemed to mirror his own sense of abandonment, his feeling of being lost in the vast, impersonal landscape of the city.

He hesitated, his fingers tracing the worn lettering. He pictured himself walking away, leaving the book exactly as he found it. The image, however, felt strangely unsatisfactory, a picture of continued stagnation. He was tired of the familiar ache in his chest, the persistent emptiness that even his solitary walks couldn't fully alleviate. He craved a change, a tangible shift in the course of his life, a chance to break free from the self-imposed prison of his own making.

The rustle of leaves, a sudden gust of wind that stirred the remaining foliage around him, seemed to push him forward. He opened the book, the pages brittle and slightly yellowed. The typeface was old-fashioned, almost elegant in its simplicity. He read the introduction, the words flowing across the page, their message both intriguing and surprisingly reassuring. It spoke of the possibility of overcoming social anxieties, of transforming one's interactions, of creating meaningful connections.

He wasn't sure if he believed it. The skepticism, ingrained deep within him, battled with a burgeoning sense of hope. He had attempted to bridge the social chasm before, and each attempt had resulted in painful failure. The sting of rejection, the awkward silences, the feeling of being an outsider were vivid and unwelcome memories. But this book, this discarded, almost forgotten tome, offered a different perspective, a different approach.

He decided to read further, a strange mix of determination and doubt stirring within him. The park, usually a symbol of his solitary existence, now held a new significance. This was the place where he found it, this forgotten guide, offering a potential path out of the solitary maze he had constructed for himself. It was a tiny spark of hope in the dim twilight of his emotional landscape. He continued reading, the crisp autumn air turning colder, but his inner world strangely warmed by the promise of change. The rustling leaves and the distant sounds of the city were a muted background to a much larger story unfolding before him – the potential transformation of a solitary life.

He sat there for a long time, absorbed in the book's contents, the fallen leaves forming a soft cushion beneath him. The chapters were concise, practical, and surprisingly easy to understand. He read about the importance of physical presence, the subtle signals that conveyed confidence and engagement, the art of asking meaningful questions. The concepts weren't revolutionary, yet they provided a framework, a concrete set of steps he could actually follow. He was drawn to the author's relatable, almost conversational tone, a stark contrast to the clinical, sometimes overly academic articles he had previously consulted.

The park itself seemed to hold its breath, as if anticipating the changes to come. The light began to fade, painting the sky in shades of purple and orange. But Gary hardly noticed. He was lost in the world the book created, a world where connections were possible, where genuine friendships could blossom. He finished the introduction, a slow smile spreading across his face. This wasn't a quick fix, a magic bullet to solve all his problems. This was a roadmap, a practical guide to navigate the complex terrain of human interaction. It wouldn't be easy, but for the first time in a long time, he felt a flicker of true, unadulterated optimism.

He closed the book, the worn cover feeling strangely comforting in his hands. He looked up, the shadows lengthening, the last vestiges of sunlight fading from the sky. He felt a sense of calm, a new kind of peace that wasn't born from solitude, but from the possibility of connection. The book wasn't just a guide to social success; it was a guide to his own potential, to a future where he wasn't just a silent observer, but an active participant, a friend, a companion. He stood up, the leaves crunching under his feet, his steps lighter than they had been in years. The lonely algorithm had found its code. He was ready to begin.

The "Top Secret Guide to Social Success" fell open to a chapter titled "Rule Number One: Physical Energy." Gary traced the faded ink with his finger, a knot of apprehension tightening in his stomach. Physical energy? It sounded...vague. He'd always considered himself a creature of quiet observation, more comfortable lurking on the periphery than thrusting himself into the chaotic dance of social interaction. The idea of projecting some sort of "energy" felt alien, almost theatrical. He pictured himself awkwardly flailing his arms, radiating an unsettling aura of forced enthusiasm. The image was less than inspiring.

He reread the first paragraph: "Your physical presence is the first impression. Before a single word is spoken, your body language, your posture, your very energy, communicates volumes about your confidence and openness to connection." He scoffed softly. Easier said than done, he thought. Confidence was a luxury he hadn't experienced in years. Openness felt like a vulnerability he guarded fiercely.

The book went on to describe the subtle yet powerful impact of posture, eye contact, and even the way one held one's hands. Gary reread those sections several times, trying to decipher the code. He learned about the power of a relaxed stance, shoulders back but not stiff, a slight tilt of the head to suggest engagement, the importance of maintaining eye contact without staring. It all felt incredibly complicated, an elaborate dance he had never been taught.

He spent the next few days attempting to integrate these concepts into his daily life. The results were, to put it mildly, disastrous. He walked around his apartment, consciously trying to adopt the "relaxed yet confident" posture advocated in the book. He looked like a marionette with tangled strings, his movements jerky and unnatural. He practiced smiling, attempting a genuine smile as opposed to his usual tight-lipped, almost apologetic grimace. It felt like he was wearing a mask, a poorly-fitted, uncomfortable mask.

Rule Number One: Physical Energy

One afternoon, he decided to take his experiment to the mirror. He spent a good hour meticulously practicing his smile, working on the subtle nuances of eye contact and hand gestures. He tried to emulate the relaxed posture described in the book, only to find himself looking stiff and awkward, a statue trying to impersonate a person. He tried different variations, and each attempt ended with him looking more ridiculous than the last. He considered giving up; it all felt utterly futile, a monumental waste of his time. He considered ripping the pages from the book.

But then, a thought struck him. The book mentioned practicing these techniques in everyday situations, however small. That day, he decided to practice his new "energy" in a real-world scenario - something as mundane as ordering coffee.

His usual coffee routine involved a mumbled order and a quick retreat. But today, armed with his newfound knowledge (or so he thought), he entered his favorite coffee shop with a newfound, although still somewhat tentative, confidence. He made eye contact with the barista, a young woman with bright, cheerful eyes, and offered a smile—a smile he consciously worked on, drawing from his mirror sessions. He even managed to relax his shoulders. He ordered his usual latte, and for the first time, instead of immediately turning away, he held the barista's gaze for a second longer than usual, offering a small nod of thanks before retreating.

As he walked out of the coffee shop, a wave of surprising relief washed over him. The small victory, the subtle shift in his demeanor, was enough. He didn't make any startling changes, nothing overly theatrical, no grand pronouncements. It was just a simple interaction, but the difference was palpable. He hadn't felt the usual crushing weight of self-consciousness, the overwhelming feeling of being scrutinized and found wanting. Instead, there was a sense of quiet accomplishment, a feeling that he had, however slightly, broken through his usual barriers.

The walk back to his apartment felt different. The familiar anxiety was still there, a faint whisper at the edge of his awareness, but it no longer dominated his thoughts. He felt a small spark of hope, a tiny flame that flickered against the vast darkness of his long-standing self-doubt. The book might have seemed absurd when he'd first found it, but now, as he continued his journey through the following chapters, he felt a growing sense of possibility. He even found himself practicing his smile on his reflection in a shop window on his way home, almost grinning at his own clumsy but earnest attempt at changing his demeanor. The journey was just beginning, but he was finally starting to walk a path that seemed to lead away from his loneliness. He looked forward to future experiments. The next chapter promised to focus on asking questions, a task he hadn't even imagined he could tackle. But with every small victory, his confidence grew, like a small seedling pushing through the hardened earth of his social anxieties.

The following week, Gary decided to apply his newfound "physical energy" – or what he now considered a slightly less disastrous approximation of it – to a slightly more challenging scenario: the local library. He'd always frequented the library, a sanctuary of quiet contemplation, but his interactions were minimal, limited to hushed exchanges with librarians. He'd never even considered striking up a conversation with a fellow patron.

This time, however, he walked in with a deliberate, if still somewhat tentative, stride. He consciously relaxed his shoulders, a tiny rebellion against the habitual hunch he'd carried for years. He found a book he wanted to browse, settling into a comfortable armchair near a window. A woman sat a few feet away, engrossed in a novel. He noticed her bright scarf, a vibrant splash of color against the muted tones of the library. A few minutes later, she paused in her reading, her gaze drifting towards the window. He made eye contact, offering a small, almost imperceptible nod. She returned the nod, a fleeting connection that felt strangely significant.

The interaction was minuscule, insignificant in the grand scheme of things, but to Gary, it was a monumental achievement. It represented a shift, a movement away from his usual passive observation towards a more active participation. He felt a surge of quiet pride, a tiny seed of confidence sprouting in the fertile soil of his self-belief. He spent the rest of his time at the library immersed in his book, but his awareness of his surroundings had changed. He noticed other readers, their absorbed expressions, the subtle rustles of turning pages. He even noticed a young boy struggling to reach a book on a high shelf. He found himself impulsively offering to help, a spontaneous act that surprised even himself.

That evening, he wrote in his journal: "Small interactions. Tiny victories. It's not about grand gestures or dazzling pronouncements. It's about these minute connections, these seemingly insignificant moments of engagement. It's about showing up, being present, not hiding in the shadows." He felt a sense of progress, a slow but steady momentum.

Small Steps & Big Changes

The following days brought further small victories. He held the door open for a stranger, exchanging a brief smile. He engaged in short, pleasant exchanges with the cashier at the grocery store, even commenting on the fresh flowers displayed near the entrance – a topic that would have previously felt wildly inappropriate and outside his comfort zone. He began to see these exchanges not as daunting challenges, but as opportunities for connection, brief moments of human interaction.

One afternoon, he found himself waiting in line at a coffee shop, a familiar setting that had once filled him with dread. He noticed a woman in front of him reading a book he recognized. He managed to muster the courage to utter a simple comment, "That's a great book. I really enjoyed it." The woman turned, her eyes widening slightly in surprise. She smiled, engaging in a short but pleasant conversation about the book before the barista called out his name. He walked away feeling a distinct lack of his usual post-interaction anxiety.

These small interactions, once sources of immense anxiety, were now opportunities to practice his newfound skills. He was no longer just passively observing; he was actively participating, even initiating conversations. The changes were subtle, almost imperceptible, but their cumulative effect was profound. His perception of himself was shifting. He was no longer the shy, withdrawn figure he had been. He was, however slowly, becoming someone more confident, more approachable, more willing to engage with the world around him.

This gradual progress was crucial. It allowed him to build confidence incrementally, celebrating each small success rather than getting overwhelmed by the enormity of his goal. The sense of accomplishment, however small, fueled his motivation, providing the impetus to continue his journey.

Gary started to notice a change in how people reacted to him. His improved posture and eye contact made him appear more approachable, inviting interaction instead of repelling it. The slightly more confident smile, once a source of anxiety, now elicited smiles in return. It wasn't a sudden transformation; it was a gradual evolution, a slow but steady shift towards a more engaged and fulfilling social life.

He still experienced moments of anxiety, of course. The familiar knot in his stomach would sometimes tighten, especially in larger social settings. But those moments were less frequent, less intense, and easier to manage. He'd learned that it was okay to feel anxious; that anxiety wasn't a sign of failure, but a natural response that could be acknowledged and navigated, not avoided. He'd learned to breathe through those moments, to ground himself, and to focus on the task at hand – whether it was ordering coffee, exchanging a few words with a library patron, or simply smiling at a stranger.

His reflections in his journal transformed from anxious self-criticism to self-encouragement. He started tracking his progress, noting the dates of his small victories, celebrating milestones like the first time he held a conversation without feeling completely overwhelmed. He documented the subtle shifts in his interactions, the lengthening of eye contact, the increased ease of his smiles, the almost imperceptible lengthening of his conversations. The journal became a chronicle of his transformation, a testament to his growing confidence and his slowly diminishing anxiety.

One evening, he found himself at a local book club meeting, something he would have previously dismissed as entirely unthinkable. He'd signed up impulsively, a leap of faith based on his accumulating small victories. The initial apprehension was still there, a lingering sense of unease, but it was significantly less overwhelming than it would have been a few months prior. He took a deep breath, reminding himself of the small steps, the gradual progress, the accumulating confidence. He actively engaged in the conversation, asking questions, sharing his thoughts, contributing to the vibrant exchange of ideas. It wasn't flawless; he still felt a touch of awkwardness, but it was manageable, even overshadowed by the thrill of participating.

As he walked home that night, a sense of profound satisfaction washed over him. He had done it. He'd attended a book club meeting, not just survived it, but actually enjoyed it. It wasn't about being perfect, about being flawlessly charismatic or effortlessly engaging. It was about showing up, about participating, about stepping out of his comfort zone and into the realm of connection. And that, more than anything, was a victory worth celebrating. He realized the importance of the journey, the small steps that, when taken consistently, led to transformative changes. The loneliness, which once seemed an insurmountable barrier, was steadily fading, replaced by a growing sense of belonging, of connection, of being part of something bigger than himself. The path ahead still held challenges, but he was no longer walking it alone. He was learning to navigate the world, step by tiny step, and with each step, his confidence grew, his anxiety diminished, and his life blossomed.

The book club meeting was a watershed moment. It wasn't just the conversation itself, though the surprisingly easy flow of discussion about Victorian literature was a welcome surprise. It was the feeling afterward, the quiet hum of satisfaction that lingered long after he'd walked home. He hadn't felt this sense of belonging, this feeling of genuine connection, in years. The loneliness that had clung to him like a shadow for so long felt…lighter. Less suffocating.

The First Friendships

The next day, he found himself thinking about the people he'd met. There was Sarah, with her infectious laugh and encyclopedic knowledge of Jane Austen; David, a quiet but insightful man who'd shared his passion for historical fiction; and Emily, whose sharp wit and insightful observations had kept the conversation lively and engaging. He found himself wanting to see them again, not out of obligation or a desperate need for social interaction, but out of a genuine desire for their company.

He cautiously reached out to Sarah, suggesting a coffee sometime. To his surprise, she readily agreed. Their first meeting was still slightly awkward, peppered with hesitant pauses and self-conscious smiles, but there was an undeniable ease that wasn't present in his previous attempts at connection. They talked about books, of course, but also about their jobs, their families (or lack thereof, in Gary's case), and their shared love of rainy days and long walks. He realized that connecting with others wasn't about flawlessly executing a rehearsed script; it was about being authentic, about sharing genuine interest and vulnerability.

The coffee date led to a second, and then a third. Soon, he found himself looking forward to these encounters, eagerly anticipating their conversations. He began to understand the power of shared interests. Talking about books wasn't just a social lubricant; it was a window into their souls, revealing shared values and passions. This was something far deeper and more meaningful than the superficial pleasantries he'd exchanged in the past.

He started applying the principles from "The Top

Secret Guide" more organically, less consciously. The physical social energy, once a calculated effort, now flowed more naturally. His posture was straighter, his smile more genuine, his eye contact more consistent. He learned to listen attentively, to ask follow-up questions, to truly engage in the conversations, not just wait for his turn to speak. His questions were no longer rote inquiries, but genuine expressions of curiosity.

His success with Sarah emboldened him to reach out to others from the book club. He and David found a shared interest in hiking, and soon they were embarking on weekend excursions, their conversations as easy and flowing as the mountain streams they traversed. With Emily, he discovered a shared passion for cooking, resulting in several friendly dinner gatherings at each other's homes.

Slowly, tentatively, Gary was building a life outside the confines of his solitude. His apartment, once a sanctuary of isolation, started to host occasional gatherings. The quiet hum of the television was sometimes replaced by the lively chatter of friends, the aroma of freshly brewed coffee mingling with the scent of homemade cookies. These gatherings were small, intimate affairs, but they were filled with warmth, laughter, and a sense of belonging that Gary had once considered unattainable.

He still had moments of self-doubt, of course. The old anxieties would occasionally surface, a faint echo of his past. But now he had tools to manage them – the techniques he'd learned from the book, the confidence gained from his successful interactions, and the support of his newfound friends. He recognized these moments of anxiety not as failures, but as opportunities to practice self-compassion and to remind himself of how far he'd come.

His journal entries, once filled with self-criticism and despair, now overflowed with gratitude and optimism. He documented his friendships, not just as a record of his progress, but as a celebration of the connections he'd forged. He described the shared laughter, the meaningful conversations, the quiet moments of companionship. These weren't just entries; they were treasures, reminders of a life transformed.

The shift wasn't sudden or dramatic. It was a gradual unfolding, a slow but steady metamorphosis from isolation to connection. Gary's transformation wasn't just about overcoming social anxiety; it was about discovering the richness and depth of human connection, about learning to embrace vulnerability, and about building a life filled with genuine friendship and belonging.

He realised that friendships weren't about grand gestures or dramatic pronouncements; they were about small acts of kindness, shared laughter, and genuine interest in another person's life. He learned to appreciate the quiet moments of companionship, the comfort of shared silence, the simple pleasure of being present in another's company.

Nine months after discovering "The Top Secret Guide to Social Success," Gary's life was vastly different. His apartment, once a symbol of his isolation, was now a vibrant hub of activity, a space where laughter echoed through the halls and warmth filled every corner. His friendships were a testament to his courage, his resilience, and his unwavering commitment to self-improvement. The loneliness that had once defined him was a distant memory, replaced by a deep sense of connection, belonging, and the profound joy of genuine human relationships. He'd learned that overcoming social anxiety wasn't about magically becoming a social butterfly overnight; it was about taking small steps, celebrating small victories, and embracing the beautiful, messy, and often unpredictable journey of human connection. And he was incredibly grateful for every step along the way. The journey hadn't been easy, but the destination – a life filled with friendship and belonging – was worth every ounce of effort.

The feeling of accomplishment wasn't just confined to his social life. His newfound confidence permeated other aspects of his existence. He started taking on new challenges at work, speaking up in meetings, and volunteering for projects that had once seemed daunting. He even joined a local choir, a venture he'd previously considered impossible.

The transformation wasn't just about overcoming social anxiety; it was about unlocking a newfound sense of self-belief and empowerment.

His increased confidence didn't erase his anxieties entirely; they still appeared occasionally, like faint shadows in the sunshine. But now, he understood them better. He knew how to manage them, to acknowledge them without allowing them to control him. The self-criticism that had once been a constant companion was replaced with self-compassion and understanding. He'd learned to be kind to himself, to celebrate his progress, and to accept that setbacks were a natural part of the journey.

One evening, while sitting with his friends in his apartment, sharing a meal and laughter, Gary looked around the room. The image was a far cry from the solitary figure he'd been nine months ago. He was surrounded by warmth, laughter, and genuine connection, something that had once seemed like a distant dream. He realized that the journey had been as important as the destination. The small steps, the incremental progress, the countless acts of courage – these were the building blocks of his transformation. And as he looked at his friends, their faces illuminated by the warm glow of the lamps, he knew that this was only the beginning of a beautiful new chapter in his life. The loneliness algorithm had been rewritten, and he was finally living the life he had always longed for.

CHAPTER 2:
THE ART OF
CONVERSATION

Mastering the Question

The book club had been a revelation, a gentle nudge into a world he'd previously deemed inaccessible. But the real challenge, as "The Top Secret Guide to Social Success" emphasized, lay in sustaining those connections, in navigating the intricacies of everyday conversation. The second golden rule, the one he was now grappling with, was perhaps the most daunting: mastering the art of asking the right questions.

Small talk, he'd discovered, was a shallow pool, offering little sustenance for genuine connection. It was the polite but ultimately meaningless exchange of pleasantries, a social lubricant that left him feeling more isolated than ever. He'd tried it countless times, the predictable questions – "How's the weather?", "What do you do?" – hanging in the air like awkward silences. The answers were equally predictable, equally unsatisfying, and left him struggling to find common ground, to forge a genuine connection.

The guide stressed the importance of moving beyond the superficial, of delving deeper, of asking questions that encouraged thoughtful responses, questions that revealed shared interests and passions. But the thought of formulating such questions filled him with trepidation. What if his questions were stupid? What if they fell flat? What if he revealed his own lack of social grace?

His anxiety was a familiar companion, a nagging voice whispering doubts and insecurities in his ear. He'd learned to recognize its presence, to acknowledge its existence without allowing it to dictate his actions. He spent hours practicing, imagining scenarios, formulating questions, and rehearsing his responses. He filled notebooks with potential conversation starters, categorizing them by topic and context. He even practiced in front of the mirror, his reflection a silent audience to his often halting, sometimes incoherent attempts.

The first real test came at a board game night, organized by one of the book club members. He'd hesitantly agreed, his heart pounding in his chest. Board games, he thought, could be a safe haven, a structured environment that minimized the risk of awkward silences. But even the structured format couldn't completely quell his anxiety.

As he arrived, he saw a group of people already gathered, their laughter echoing through the room. He felt a familiar surge of self-doubt, the urge to turn around and retreat to the safety of his apartment. But he pushed through, reminding himself of the progress he'd made, the confidence he'd cultivated. He took a deep breath, straightened his posture, and forced a smile.

The game itself was a distraction, a welcome diversion from his inner turmoil. But as the game ended, and conversations began to flow naturally around the table, Gary found himself facing the challenge head-on. His first attempt was tentative, a cautious inquiry about someone's favorite game. The response was polite but rather generic. He realized he needed to be more specific, more insightful.

He shifted his approach, focusing on asking open-ended questions that couldn't be answered with a simple "yes" or "no." Instead of asking, "Do you like strategy games?", he tried, "What do you find most appealing about strategy games?" The difference was remarkable. The response was much more detailed, revealing a wealth of information about the person's preferences, their personality, their interests.

The conversation continued, moving seamlessly from board games to hobbies, books, travel, and dreams. He asked about their favorite travel destinations, not just where they'd been, but what they loved about those places – the people, the culture, the experiences. He probed their passion for certain hobbies, seeking to understand not only the activity itself, but also the emotional connection they felt to it.

With each insightful question, he felt his confidence growing, his anxieties receding. He realized that the art of conversation wasn't about perfectly formulated questions; it was about genuine curiosity, about a sincere desire to understand the other person. He listened attentively, not just waiting for his turn to speak, but actively engaging in what the other person was saying, asking follow-up questions that showed his interest and understanding.

One woman, a graphic designer named Lisa, shared her passion for art and her struggles with creative blocks. Gary, remembering his own struggles with writer's block, could relate to her experiences. He asked her about her creative process, her sources of inspiration, and the techniques she used to overcome her challenges. The conversation flowed easily, effortlessly, marked by shared experiences and mutual understanding.

Another participant, Mark, a software engineer, spoke passionately about his work on a new app. Gary, having little knowledge of software engineering, asked him questions not just about the technical aspects of the app, but also about the problem it solved, the people it was designed for, and the challenges of bringing it to fruition. He learned not only about Mark's work, but also about his problem-solving skills, his creativity, and his dedication.

The board game night was a triumph, a testament to Gary's progress. He found himself engaged in meaningful conversations, creating connections that went beyond
superficial pleasantries. He wasn't just asking questions; he was building relationships, fostering understanding, and discovering shared interests.

As the night wound down, he felt a sense of accomplishment he hadn't experienced before. He realized the key wasn't just about asking the right questions, but about approaching conversations with a genuine desire to connect, with an open heart and an inquisitive mind. He'd learned to listen as intently as he spoke, to engage with others on a deeper level, to find common ground, to share his own experiences without fear of judgment.

He left the board game night feeling energized, empowered, and excited about the prospect of future social interactions. He wasn't yet a social butterfly, but he was no longer the shy, withdrawn man he once was. He was becoming someone comfortable in his own skin, someone confident in his ability to connect with others. He understood that the process was iterative, a continuous cycle of learning, practicing, and refining his skills. The more he practiced the art of asking the right questions, the more confident he became, and the more effortless the conversations flowed.

The "Top Secret Guide to Social Success" hadn't provided a magic formula, but a framework, a roadmap for navigating the complex landscape of social interaction. The book had given him tools and techniques, but it was his own commitment, his perseverance, and his willingness to step outside his comfort zone that had truly transformed his life. The journey was far from over, but he was no longer afraid to embark on the next chapter of his social adventures. His newfound confidence was a powerful weapon, enabling him to tackle even the most daunting social situations with courage and grace. He was becoming the person he always knew he could be.

The book club, once a daunting prospect, now felt like a familiar comfort. But the "Top Secret Guide" emphasized the need to extend beyond these structured settings, to navigate the unpredictable currents of everyday social interaction. This meant venturing into the less predictable waters of casual encounters, where the carefully constructed scaffolding of a pre-arranged event was absent.

Beyond Small Talk – Gary Speaks

My first experiment was at the local coffee shop, a place I'd previously avoided like the plague. Armed with my newfound understanding of open-ended questions and active listening, I took a deep breath and ordered my usual latte. I noticed a woman sitting alone, engrossed in a book. The title, "One Hundred Years of Solitude," piqued my interest. Instead of the usual anxiety-fueled avoidance, I found myself drawn towards her.

Approaching her, I felt a familiar tremor of anxiety, but this time, it was a manageable hum rather than a deafening roar. I started tentatively, "That's quite a book you're reading. I've always meant to read it, but never got around to it. What's drawing you into it?"

Her response surprised me. She wasn't dismissive or curt; instead, she spoke passionately about the book's magical realism, its exploration of family dynamics, and the author's masterful storytelling. I listened intently, not just hearing her words, but observing her subtle gestures, the slight crinkle of her eyes when she described a particularly moving passage. This wasn't about memorizing questions; it was about genuine curiosity, a sincere desire to understand her perspective.

Our conversation meandered effortlessly from Gabriel García Márquez to our shared love for historical fiction, then to our contrasting approaches to reading – she preferred the immersive experience of a physical book, while I often opted for the convenience of ebooks. It was a simple conversation, yet it felt profoundly different from anything I'd experienced before. It was a genuine connection built on shared interests, not forced pleasantries.

The key, I realized, wasn't just about asking the right questions but also about actively listening. The guide had stressed the importance of mirroring and matching – subtly adopting the other person's body language and speech patterns to build rapport. With this woman, I noticed her calm demeanor and measured speech; I unconsciously slowed my own pace, mirroring her relaxed posture. This subtle mirroring fostered a sense of connection, creating a shared rhythm in our interaction.

Emboldened by my success at the coffee shop, I began experimenting in other settings. I struck up conversations with people at the park, at the grocery store, even while waiting in line at the post office. Each interaction, though seemingly insignificant, honed my conversational skills, strengthening my confidence. I learned that meaningful conversations could blossom anywhere, anytime, provided I approached them with an open mind and a genuine interest in the other person.

One afternoon, while waiting for a bus, I overheard two men discussing a local art exhibition. I cautiously joined their conversation, asking them about their favorite pieces. Their enthusiasm was infectious, and soon, we were engaged in a lively exchange about modern art, artistic expression, and the role of art in society. Again, I focused on active listening, asking follow-up questions to show my engagement. This conversation wasn't just about art; it was about shared appreciation, about connecting with others through a common interest.

Another time, I struck up a conversation with a woman at a farmers' market, simply by complimenting her beautiful bouquet of sunflowers. This led to a discussion about gardening, her passion for organic produce, and the joys and challenges of cultivating her own backyard garden. These interactions, once terrifying prospects, now felt empowering, fostering a sense of connection and belonging.

The "Top Secret Guide" hadn't provided a magic wand to instantly erase my social anxiety. Instead, it provided a roadmap, a series of tools and techniques that, when applied consistently, yielded remarkable results. The consistent practice of open-ended questioning, active listening, and subtle mirroring helped me build genuine connections with people from all walks of life. I was no longer merely participating in conversations; I was actively building bridges of understanding and forging meaningful relationships.

My transformation wasn't merely a matter of adopting specific conversational techniques; it was a profound shift in my mindset. I had learned to see conversations not as daunting challenges but as opportunities for connection, for learning, and for personal growth. The genuine curiosity I cultivated transformed my interactions from superficial exchanges to engaging dialogues that enriched my life in countless ways.

The key wasn't about mastering the perfect question or the ideal response; it was about approaching each conversation with a sincere desire to connect, to understand, and to share. It was about stepping out of my self-imposed isolation and embracing the richness and diversity of human connection. My journey wasn't a linear progression, but rather an iterative process of learning, experimenting, and refining my skills. There were still moments of anxiety, moments when my old habits resurfaced, but my newfound confidence and skills allowed me to navigate those moments with greater resilience and self-awareness.

My newfound skills extended beyond casual encounters. I found myself contributing more actively to the book club discussions, engaging in more profound exchanges with my fellow members. Conversations that once felt strained and awkward now flowed naturally, filled with genuine interest and shared experiences. The transformation was not only in my conversational skills but in my overall approach to social interaction. I was no longer a passive observer, clinging to the periphery; I was an active participant, engaging fully in the ebb and flow of social life. My life, once defined by isolation and loneliness, had become vibrant and meaningful, filled with genuine connections and lasting friendships. The "Top Secret Guide" had provided the framework, but it was my own commitment, my persistence, and my willingness to step outside my comfort zone that had truly transformed my life. The journey was ongoing, a continuous adventure in self-discovery and human connection. And I was ready for it, eager to embrace the next chapter, the next conversation, the next connection.

But mastering the art of conversation, as the "Top Secret Guide" so eloquently pointed out, wasn't solely about asking the right questions. It was about something far more profound: active listening. This wasn't merely hearing the words; it was about absorbing the essence of the message, understanding the unspoken nuances, and responding with genuine empathy. The guide emphasized the importance of nonverbal cues – the subtle shifts in posture, the fleeting expressions, the almost imperceptible changes in tone – all whispering a story beneath the surface of spoken words.

Active Listening: A Deeper Dive

My initial attempts at active listening were clumsy, halting. I'd nod enthusiastically, offering the occasional "uh-huh" or "that's interesting," but my mind often drifted, preoccupied with formulating my next question, my next witty remark. I was listening to respond, not listening to understand.

The "Top Secret Guide" called this "pseudo-listening," a superficial imitation of genuine engagement.

The guide offered a simple yet powerful technique: mirroring and matching. This wasn't about mimicking someone's every move, but about subtly reflecting their body language and pace of speech. If someone spoke slowly and deliberately, I would adjust my own speech to match their rhythm. If they leaned forward, I would subtly mirror the gesture, creating a sense of synchronicity, a shared rhythm in our interaction. This technique, the guide explained, unconsciously fostered a sense of connection, creating a feeling of rapport and trust.

I practiced this technique diligently, initially feeling self-conscious and awkward. But with each successful interaction, my confidence grew. I learned to observe subtle cues – a furrowed brow indicating concern, a slight smile hinting at amusement, a hesitant pause revealing uncertainty. These observations weren't just about deciphering the message; they were about connecting with the person on a deeper level, understanding their emotional landscape.

One evening, while attending a poetry reading, I struck up a conversation with a woman who was visibly moved by one of the poems. Instead of offering a generic compliment, I observed her tear-filled eyes and the slight tremor in her voice. I asked her gently, "That poem clearly resonated with you. Would you mind sharing what touched you so deeply?"

Her response was heartfelt, a poignant reflection on her own experiences, revealing a vulnerability that I wouldn't have witnessed if I hadn't been paying close attention to her nonverbal cues. As she shared her story, I mirrored her subdued tone and posture, creating a safe space for her to express her emotions. Our conversation lasted far longer than I anticipated, a genuine exchange built on empathy and understanding, not forced pleasantries.

Another instance involved a chance encounter with an elderly gentleman in the park. He was feeding pigeons, a melancholic expression etched on his face. I sat beside him, listening intently as he shared stories of his late wife, his voice filled with both sadness and fond memories. I didn't interrupt, didn't offer platitudes; I simply listened, offering occasional nods and empathetic murmurs to show my understanding. Our conversation transcended the usual superficial exchanges, evolving into a shared moment of remembrance and reflection.

The "Top Secret Guide" also emphasized the importance of avoiding interruptions. This required a conscious effort to resist the urge to jump in with my own thoughts or experiences. I practiced the art of patient listening, allowing the other person to complete their thoughts without interruption, creating space for genuine dialogue.

This involved consciously resisting the urge to plan my next question while someone was still speaking. Instead of racing ahead mentally, I focused intently on what was being said, allowing myself to be fully present in the moment. This practice greatly enhanced my ability to comprehend the nuances of the conversation and to respond with thoughtful, relevant remarks.

I discovered that active listening was more than just a technique; it was a mindset. It was about approaching each interaction with genuine curiosity, a sincere desire to understand the other person's perspective, regardless of whether I agreed with their views. This approach fostered a sense of mutual respect, transforming superficial encounters into meaningful dialogues.

One significant improvement was my ability to ask relevant follow-up questions.
These weren't merely surface-level queries; they were thoughtfully crafted inquiries designed to delve deeper into the conversation, demonstrating my genuine interest. This showed the other person that I valued their input, that their thoughts and experiences were truly heard and appreciated.

This refined approach greatly enhanced my interactions, leading to more meaningful connections. My conversations were no longer fleeting exchanges but genuine dialogues, filled with shared experiences and mutual understanding. The shift was palpable. People responded more openly, sharing more of themselves than they might have otherwise. I was no longer merely participating in conversations; I was actively building bridges of understanding, fostering a sense of connection and belonging.

Active listening, I discovered, was a powerful tool for resolving conflicts as well. In one instance, a disagreement arose in the book club regarding the interpretation of a particular passage. Instead of immediately stating my own viewpoint, I actively listened to the different perspectives, ensuring each member felt heard and understood. This empathetic approach facilitated a constructive dialogue, ultimately leading to a shared understanding and a resolution that satisfied everyone.

Building Rapport

The success I found in applying active listening went beyond my personal interactions. It extended to my professional life, enhancing my working relationships and improving my team collaborations. By actively listening to colleagues' opinions and perspectives, I could better understand their concerns and work collaboratively to achieve shared goals. This resulted in increased efficiency, improved teamwork, and a more positive and productive work environment.

As the months progressed, the impact of active listening became increasingly evident. My social interactions had evolved from tentative, anxiety-ridden encounters to confident, engaging dialogues. I was no longer a passive observer on the periphery of social gatherings, but an active participant, fully engaged in the ebb and flow of conversation. My social anxiety, once a debilitating force, had gradually diminished, replaced by a growing sense of confidence and belonging.

The "Top Secret Guide" had unlocked a key that had been hidden from my view for so long. It wasn't just about mastering the art of conversation; it was about the mastery of human connection, a journey of continuous learning and growth. My transformation wasn't just about acquiring new skills, but about cultivating a deeper understanding of myself and my relationship with the world.

The journey continued, a process of refinement, of fine-tuning my ability to connect with others on a deeper level. I continued to practice active listening, consistently honing my skills, aware that the journey of social connection is an ongoing process of discovery and growth. The once daunting task of navigating social situations had become an opportunity to learn, to connect, and to deepen my understanding of the human experience. This wasn't merely about mastering conversations; it was about mastering the art of human connection, and I was finally well on my way.

But the "Top Secret Guide" went beyond simply listening; it delved into the art of *building rapport*, a skill far more nuanced than I'd initially imagined.

It wasn't a one-size-fits-all approach, the guide stressed. Connecting with a boisterous comedian required a different tactic than engaging with a quiet artist, or a sharp-witted professor. The key, it turned out, was adaptability—a chameleon-like ability to shift my communication style to resonate with the individual I was interacting with.

My first attempts at this were, to put it mildly, disastrous. I tried mimicking the booming laugh of the comedian, ending up sounding like a strangled goose. With the artist, my attempts at quiet contemplation morphed into awkward silence. The professor, accustomed to intellectual sparring, found my hesitant attempts at mirroring his precise language to be irritatingly stilted. It was a humbling experience, a stark reminder that genuine connection stemmed not from imitation, but from genuine understanding and respect.

The guide suggested a simple framework: observation, adaptation, and authenticity. Observation, it explained, wasn't just about passively watching; it involved actively noting the individual's body language, their speech patterns, their overall demeanor. Was their energy high or low? Were they expressive or reserved? Did they favour direct communication or indirect cues? These observations, the guide emphasized, were the foundation upon which to build a tailored approach.

Adaptation involved consciously adjusting my communication style to complement theirs. If someone was highly energetic, I would match their enthusiasm, my tone and pace mirroring theirs. With more reserved individuals, I would adopt a calmer, more measured approach, allowing the conversation to unfold naturally at their pace. This wasn't about changing who I was fundamentally, but about finding a common rhythm, a shared wavelength that facilitated easy communication. It was about creating a sense of comfort and ease, allowing the other person to feel understood and appreciated.

Authenticity was the crucial element that held it all together. The guide warned against inauthentic mimicry, against trying to be someone I wasn't. The goal wasn't to impress, but to connect genuinely. My adapted style had to feel natural, an extension of my true self, not a forced performance. This authenticity, I discovered, was what gave my interactions depth and meaning, what allowed the other person to sense my genuine interest and respect.

I practiced this framework diligently. At the local farmers market, I struck up a conversation with a gruff-looking farmer selling heirloom tomatoes. Observing his strong, deliberate movements and his straightforward manner, I adopted a similar direct style. I asked about his farming techniques, his voice calm and respectful, avoiding unnecessary embellishments. Our conversation was short but meaningful, a genuine exchange devoid of forced pleasantries. He seemed to appreciate my genuine interest, ending up sharing stories of his family's legacy with the farm.

Conversely, at a book club meeting, I engaged with a shy, introspective woman. Observing her quiet demeanor and thoughtful expressions, I adopted a slower, gentler approach. Instead of dominating the conversation, I listened attentively, allowing her to express her thoughts without interruption. Our conversation blossomed organically, a shared exploration of literary themes, a connection forged not through boisterous pronouncements but through quiet understanding.

The contrast between these interactions highlighted the importance of adaptability. The farmer valued directness, while the book club member appreciated quiet contemplation. Trying to apply the same communication style to both would have been a recipe for disaster. The success I experienced lay in my ability to observe, adapt, and connect authentically, recognizing that each person was unique and deserving of a tailored approach.

The Ripple Effect

My interactions started to become richer, more nuanced. Conversations with colleagues at work evolved from strained professional exchanges to genuine dialogues. I found that by actively observing their communication styles, adjusting mine accordingly, and approaching each interaction with genuine interest, I could build stronger working relationships, improving team cohesion and project effectiveness.

I also started applying this principle to my personal relationships. I noticed that my conversations with my family members, previously fraught with misunderstandings, began to improve. By observing their unique communication styles and adjusting mine, I could connect with them on a deeper level. This led to a stronger sense of intimacy and mutual understanding.

One particularly rewarding instance involved a chance encounter with a street musician. His music was captivating, his performance raw and emotionally charged. Observing his passionate energy and expressive movements, I matched his enthusiasm, engaging him in a conversation about his music, his influences, and his aspirations. Our conversation was electric, a vibrant exchange of energy and ideas. He invited me to attend his next performance, a gesture that resonated with the genuine connection we had forged.

As I continued to hone my skills in building rapport, I noticed a shift in my own self-perception. My anxiety, once a significant barrier to social interaction, began to recede. This wasn't because I was suddenly a master of social manipulation, but because I had discovered the profound power of genuine connection. I was no longer afraid of awkward silences or misinterpretations;

I approached each interaction with a sense of curiosity and respect, ready to adapt and learn, and confident in my ability to connect with others on a meaningful level. The journey continued, but I was walking with surer steps, feeling increasingly at ease and at home in the world of human interaction.

The "Top Secret Guide" hadn't provided a magic formula, but a set of principles, a framework for understanding the art of human connection. It emphasized the importance of observation, the flexibility of adaptation, and the unwavering necessity of authenticity. This wasn't merely about improving my conversational skills; it was about enhancing my ability to relate to and understand other people, fostering genuine empathy and a deeper sense of belonging. It had changed not just my social life, but my entire outlook on life. The world felt less daunting, more connected, and filled with the possibility of meaningful interactions.

Nine months after my initial discovery of the book, I found myself surrounded by friends, colleagues, and acquaintances. The transformation had been gradual, but undeniable. I wasn't simply attending social events; I was actively participating, contributing meaningfully, and enjoying the richness of genuine human connection. The lonely man who had once existed on the periphery of life had, through the practice of active listening and the art of building rapport, found his place at the heart of the social world. My journey wasn't just a success story; it was a testament to the power of self-improvement and the transformative effects of genuine human connection. The once daunting task of navigating social situations had become a journey of discovery, a constant learning process enriching my life in ways I could hardly have imagined. The "Top Secret Guide" wasn't just a book; it was a roadmap to a richer, more fulfilling life.

The ripple effect of my newfound social skills was astonishing. It wasn't just about having more friends; it was a complete overhaul of how I interacted with the world. My confidence, once a fragile seedling, blossomed into a sturdy oak, its branches reaching into every aspect of my life.

At work, the change was dramatic. Previously, team meetings had been exercises in anxiety, filled with the dread of speaking up, the fear of saying the wrong thing. I'd often retreat into silence, a ghost in the room, contributing little to the discussions. Now, however, I found myself actively participating, offering suggestions, engaging in debates, and even leading some brainstorming sessions. My colleagues, initially surprised by my transformation, quickly embraced my newfound assertiveness. My contributions proved valuable, and the team dynamics improved significantly. Project deadlines were met with greater efficiency, and the overall atmosphere became more collaborative and positive. My improved communication wasn't just about expressing my own ideas; it allowed me to understand and appreciate the perspectives of my colleagues, fostering a deeper sense of camaraderie. The once daunting professional environment felt less like a battlefield and more like a collaborative endeavor.

The impact extended beyond the workplace. My interactions with my family, long marked by misunderstandings and strained conversations, began to improve dramatically. I applied the same principles of observation, adaptation, and authenticity that had served me so well in my friendships. I listened more attentively, actively seeking to understand their perspectives, even when I disagreed. I adjusted my communication style to match their individual preferences, speaking directly with my pragmatic father and engaging in more nuanced conversations with my emotionally expressive mother. Even my younger sister, who once viewed me as the awkward older brother, began to open up, revealing her anxieties and concerns, and creating a newfound depth to our relationship. These improved communication patterns were not merely a change in conversational technique; they represented a transformation in our relationships, resulting in a deeper sense of connection and understanding within the family dynamic.

This newfound confidence even extended to my relationship with myself. I had always been my own harshest critic, constantly second-guessing my actions and agonizing over past mistakes. This self-doubt, however, began to fade as I experienced the positive outcomes of my improved social skills. I realized that my worth wasn't determined by the approval of others, but by my ability to be authentic and genuine in my interactions. This newfound self-acceptance wasn't just a feeling; it became a solid foundation for confidence, giving me the strength to take on new challenges both personally and professionally. The previously overwhelming weight of self-criticism was lifted, replaced by a sense of self-assuredness and well-being that permeated all areas of my life.

One particularly rewarding experience arose from an unexpected quarter. A friend, Sarah, confided in me about her own struggles with social anxiety. She described the same feelings of isolation and inadequacy that had once plagued me, the same crippling fear of social interaction. Hearing her words brought me back to my own past, to the loneliness and despair that had defined my life before discovering the "Top Secret Guide." I saw in her a reflection of my former self, a reminder of how far I had come.

And that's when I knew I had to help her. Drawing on my own experiences, I shared the principles I had learned—the importance of observation, adaptation, and authenticity, the power of genuine connection. I didn't offer quick fixes or magic solutions; rather, I shared my own journey, the setbacks I had faced, and the small victories that had led to my transformation. I helped her develop her own strategies, tailored to her individual personality and circumstances. We practiced active listening exercises, role-played social interactions, and discussed how to navigate challenging social situations.

This mentorship wasn't just about helping Sarah; it was a profound experience for me. In guiding her through her journey, I reinforced my own understanding of the principles I had learned, solidifying my own progress and strengthening my commitment to my social growth. It was a testament to how far I had come, from a lonely man struggling to navigate social interactions to someone who could confidently guide and support others. The satisfaction I derived from helping Sarah was immense, a sense of accomplishment that transcended the mere acquisition of social skills. This was about making a tangible difference in someone's life, about sharing the knowledge that had so profoundly transformed my own.

The experience reaffirmed the holistic nature of social skill development. It wasn't just about mastering the art of conversation; it was about building confidence, fostering empathy, and creating meaningful connections. The impact extended far beyond individual interactions, influencing my relationships with family, friends, and colleagues. The transformation I had undergone was a testament to the power of self-improvement, the profound impact of genuine human connection, and the ripple effect of a single decision to change. The "Top Secret Guide" wasn't just a book; it was a catalyst for a profound and lasting transformation, shaping not only my own life, but also influencing the lives of others. My journey had become more than a personal success; it had become an opportunity to inspire and uplift others facing similar challenges, a demonstration that overcoming social anxiety and building meaningful connections was not only possible, but deeply rewarding. The world felt different now; it felt connected, vibrant, and full of possibilities. The solitary journey had led me to a place of connection, and that is where true success lay.

The nine months since my initial discovery of the "Top Secret Guide" felt like a lifetime ago. The man who started this journey, a shadow clinging to the edges of social situations, felt like a distant stranger. He was timid, unsure, burdened by the fear of rejection and loneliness. Yet here I was, confident and connected, a testament to the transformative power of self-improvement and the principles of the guide. The journey wasn't over; social interactions, like life itself, are dynamic, ever-evolving. But I knew I had the tools, the resilience, and the courage to continue navigating this wonderful, sometimes challenging world of human connection. And more importantly, I had found my place within it; not just on the fringes, but at the very heart. The ripple effect of my transformation had gone far beyond my own life, and that, more than anything, was the greatest reward. It was a testament to the interconnectedness of human experience and a reminder of the profound impact that a single act of self-improvement could have on the world. The lonely man was gone; in his place stood someone stronger, more confident, and more profoundly connected. And that, I realised, was a success story worth sharing.

CHAPTER 3: STEPPING INTO THE SOCIAL SPOTLIGHT

Conquering the Social Event

The invitation to Sarah's birthday party had initially sent a jolt of anxiety through me. A large gathering, a sea of unfamiliar faces – it was the kind of event I would have previously avoided at all costs. But this time felt different. The "Top Secret Guide" had equipped me with a new set of tools, a newfound confidence that whispered, "You've got this." I still felt a flutter of nerves, a familiar tremor in my hands, but it was manageable, a mere whisper compared to the roaring storm of anxiety that would have consumed me just months ago.

As I approached the house, music pulsed through the walls, a vibrant rhythm that promised energy and excitement. I took a deep breath, consciously adjusting my posture – shoulders back, head held high, a smile playing on my lips – the physical embodiment of the book's first principle: mastering physical social energy. This wasn't just about body language; it was about projecting confidence, about owning the space I occupied.

Stepping inside, I was immediately enveloped by a wave of sound and movement. Laughter, music, and the murmur of conversations created a vibrant tapestry of human interaction. The initial surge of sensory overload threatened to overwhelm me, a flashback to my former self. But I anchored myself, remembering the book's advice: observe, adapt, participate.

I started by observing. I scanned the room, taking in the dynamics of the groups, the flow of conversations, the subtle cues of body language. I noticed small clusters of people engaged in animated discussions, others gathered around food tables, and some individuals standing alone, seemingly observing as I once did. This observation wasn't passive; it was strategic, helping me choose my entry point.

I spotted a small group near the refreshment table, their conversation punctuated by laughter. The "Top Secret Guide" had emphasized the importance of choosing the right questions to initiate conversations, questions that were open-ended and engaging, sparking further discussion rather than leading to simple yes or no answers.

Approaching them with a smile, I decided on my approach. "Wow, this punch is amazing," I began, keeping my tone light and friendly. "What's everyone's favorite thing about Sarah?" This wasn't merely a statement; it was an invitation, a subtle way to integrate myself into their conversation.

Their faces lit up, and they readily responded. One person mentioned Sarah's infectious laugh, another her incredible kindness, and a third her unwavering support during challenging times. Their responses gave me opportunities to engage further. I listened attentively, offering my own anecdotes about Sarah, demonstrating my connection to the group without oversharing. The conversation flowed naturally, fueled by shared experiences and genuine interest in each other. The fear I had initially felt dissipated completely, replaced by a sense of ease and belonging.

Later in the evening, I found myself engaged in a conversation about travel. A woman named Emily shared her passion for backpacking through Southeast Asia. Instead of simply listening, I drew upon my own limited travel experiences, sharing a short anecdote about a memorable trip I'd taken years ago. This wasn't about boasting; it was about creating a connection, demonstrating shared interests, and building rapport. It revealed a shared love for the unexpected adventures life offered, rather than focusing only on the destinations themselves. We discussed the challenges and rewards of independent travel, the unexpected friendships formed along the way, and the lessons learned from venturing outside of our comfort zones.

Another conversation unfolded with a man named David who was discussing his love of classic literature. My initial response, a genuine expression of my own appreciation for certain authors, opened a fascinating discussion about the power of storytelling, its ability to transport us to different worlds and offer insights into the human condition. Our conversation didn't solely revolve around specific books or authors; rather, it expanded to include our personal interpretation of stories, the impact stories had on shaping our lives, and how stories can become a way to connect with our past, present and future selves. The conversation transcended a mere discussion about books; it became a deeper exploration of life's experiences.

Throughout the evening, I applied the principles of the "Top Secret Guide," consciously managing my physical energy, asking thoughtful questions, and actively participating in the conversations. I found myself drawn into various discussions, seamlessly transitioning between groups, always mindful of maintaining a balance between engagement and observing. I paid attention to the body language of those I interacted with, making sure not to dominate the conversation, offering encouragement to others who appeared to be a bit withdrawn. I listened more than I spoke, but when I did speak, my words carried weight, reflecting my newfound confidence and clarity of thought.

The party wasn't a performance; it was a genuine experience. I wasn't pretending to be someone I wasn't; rather, I was revealing the true self, a self that had emerged from the shadows of anxiety and found its voice. The confidence I exuded was not a mask, but an authentic reflection of the growth I had achieved.

As the party wound down, I felt a profound sense of accomplishment. It wasn't just about the number of people I had spoken to; it was about the quality of those interactions, the connections I had forged, and the confidence I had demonstrated. This was the culmination of months of effort, a testament to the transformative power of the "Top Secret Guide."

Leaving the party, the music fading into the background, I felt no anxiety, no exhaustion, only a quiet sense of fulfillment. The principles I had learned weren't just theoretical concepts; they were tools that had allowed me to navigate a previously daunting social environment with ease and confidence.

This wasn't just about conquering a single social event. It was about conquering a lifelong fear, a fear that had held me captive for far too long. The party was a significant milestone, a symbol of the progress I had made, a testament to the power of self-improvement and the transformative potential within me.

The memories of the night—the laughter, the engaging conversations, the shared moments of connection—became a powerful reinforcement of the progress I'd made. Each conversation, each interaction served as a building block in my journey toward greater social confidence and well-being. The party wasn't merely a social event; it was a personal victory. It was a culmination of the knowledge I'd learned and the hard work I'd put in, manifesting as a clear demonstration of my personal transformation and the effectiveness of the "Top Secret Guide". The once-daunting prospect of social interaction had been conquered, not through avoidance or avoidance, but through embracing the challenge head-on, armed with new skills and strategies that had transformed my understanding of myself and my place in the world.

I realized that overcoming social anxiety wasn't about eliminating all feelings of nervousness; it was about learning to manage those feelings, to understand them as a natural part of the human experience, and to harness them to fuel my determination rather than allowing them to dictate my actions.

The following days were filled with a quiet satisfaction. The experience was far more than just attending a party. It was about reclaiming control over my social life, and a demonstration of my ability to engage in the world in a way I never thought possible.

The insights I gained from each conversation, from the shared laughter to the deeper discussions about life and personal experiences, solidified my confidence. Each interaction had reinforced the positive ripple effects of my newfound self-assurance and social grace. The experience at Sarah's party resonated with me long after the music had faded and the guests had departed. It served as a powerful reminder of how far I'd come, a testament to my ability to challenge myself, push past my comfort zone, and step into the social spotlight with grace and confidence.

The confidence I felt after Sarah's party wasn't a fleeting high; it was a foundation upon which I could build. The "Top Secret Guide" hadn't just provided me with a set of tools; it had ignited a fire within me, a desire to actively participate in life, to no longer remain on the sidelines. The third rule —active participation—was no longer a theoretical concept; it was a way of life.

Active Participation

My first foray into active participation was less glamorous than a birthday party. It was a volunteer event at a local animal shelter, cleaning kennels and playing with the cats. Initially, the thought of interacting with strangers while performing menial tasks filled me with a familiar pang of anxiety. But I channeled the newfound confidence I'd cultivated, reminding myself that this wasn't about socializing for the sake of socializing; it was about contributing, about making a difference, and, in a way, about connecting with something beyond myself.

The experience was surprisingly rewarding. The shared purpose of caring for the animals created an immediate sense of camaraderie. I found myself chatting with other volunteers, effortlessly engaging in conversations about the animals, their personalities, and our shared passion for animal welfare. These interactions weren't forced; they were genuine, born from a shared activity and a shared purpose. The conversations were simple, focused on the tasks at hand and the animals in our care, yet they built a connection nonetheless. I learned about a volunteer named Jessica who was a veterinarian student, her insights into animal behavior proving both informative and engaging. I shared a funny anecdote about a particularly mischievous kitten, sparking laughter and a sense of shared understanding. The work was physically demanding, but the emotional rewards far outweighed any physical exertion. That day, I wasn't just overcoming social anxiety; I was discovering a fulfilling sense of purpose.

Emboldened by this success, I decided to tackle a challenge that would have previously seemed insurmountable: joining a recreational sports team.

The idea of competing, of potentially making mistakes in front of others, had always been a source of intense anxiety. But the "Top Secret Guide" had taught me that embracing vulnerability was key to growth. I joined a beginner's basketball team, fully aware that my skills were far from polished.

The initial practices were nerve-wracking. I fumbled passes, missed shots, and often felt self-conscious about my lack of experience. But the team was incredibly welcoming. My teammates' encouragement, their focus on teamwork and improvement, created a supportive and inclusive atmosphere. I actively participated in team discussions, offering my suggestions and openly acknowledging my areas for improvement. I discovered that my anxiety wasn't a barrier to participation; it was a motivator, driving me to practice harder and improve my skills.

Games were initially a source of stress, but as I became more comfortable with the team and my abilities, the anxiety lessened. The focus shifted from self-doubt to the thrill of the game. I learned to celebrate both victories and defeats as opportunities for growth and learning. Winning games boosted confidence, while losses prompted honest self-reflection and a renewed commitment to practice.

Moreover, basketball became a fantastic opportunity to connect with people outside the structured context of conversations. The shared physical exertion, the strategic discussions during time-outs, and even the post-game celebrations fostered a unique sense of camaraderie. The conversations weren't always profound; they were often centered on the game itself, strategies, or funny moments on the court. But the shared experiences of striving for a common goal created a bond stronger than any casual conversation. The easy banter after a game, the shared pizza slices, and the casual jokes exchanged on the bench solidified a sense of belonging.

Beyond organized activities, I began to incorporate active participation into my daily life. I initiated conversations with shopkeepers, engaged in small talk with neighbors, and even struck up conversations with fellow commuters. These seemingly insignificant interactions were significant steps in my journey. They were reminders that connecting with others wasn't a daunting task; it was a natural human experience.

One particularly memorable interaction was with a barista at my local coffee shop. Every morning, I would go to the coffee shop and engage in a brief conversation, always remembering to ask open-ended questions to spark a further discussion. The initial small talk developed into genuine conversations, encompassing everything from his passion for art to his plans for a trip to Italy. These exchanges, initially feeling contrived and forced, transformed into real connections, a demonstration of how genuine engagement can lead to unexpected friendships. The casual chats became a welcoming start to my day, a reminder that even mundane routines could be infused with meaningful human connection.

I even started attending local events, from art walks to farmer's markets. I made a conscious effort to engage with vendors, asking questions about their products, sharing my opinions, and expressing my appreciation for their work. These simple interactions, far from being intimidating, were often met with warmth and enthusiasm. The shared interests around local art, agriculture, or even simply the weather created an immediate sense of community.

The progress I made wasn't linear. There were days when anxiety still crept in, days when I felt the urge to retreat into my shell. But the "Top Secret Guide's" principles had become ingrained in me. I learned to recognize those feelings, to acknowledge them without judgment, and to use them as a signal to consciously employ the tools I had acquired.

Nine Months Later

Nine months after discovering the "Top Secret Guide," my life was unrecognizable. The lonely existence I had once known was a distant memory. I had built genuine connections, forged friendships, and discovered a sense of belonging. The anxiety still lingered occasionally, a faint whisper instead of a roaring storm. But I had learned to manage it, to channel it into positive action, and to use it as fuel for my continued growth. My journey wasn't about eliminating anxiety entirely; it was about learning to live alongside it, to use it as a catalyst for change, and to redefine my relationship with the world around me. I had learned that active participation wasn't just about attending events or joining groups; it was about actively engaging with life, with people, and with myself. It was about embracing vulnerability, celebrating imperfections, and understanding that connection and growth were ongoing processes, not destinations to be reached. The transformation wasn't just about social skills, but about fostering genuine human connection, leading to a richer, more fulfilling life. The once-intimidating social world had become a place of discovery, a canvas on which I was painting a new and exciting self-portrait, one brushstroke of meaningful connection at a time.

The animal shelter had been a revelation, a gentle introduction to the power of shared experiences. But I craved something more, something that pushed me further beyond my comfort zone. The "Top Secret Guide" spoke of shared experiences as the bedrock of strong relationships, and I was ready to test its wisdom. My next venture was a weekend camping trip, an idea that would have sent shivers down my spine just months before. The thought of spending an entire weekend in the wilderness, surrounded by people I barely knew, was initially terrifying. But the prospect of a shared adventure, of overcoming a challenge together, outweighed my anxiety.

The group consisted of people I'd met through the basketball team and the volunteer work. There was Jessica, the veterinary student; Mark, a jovial software engineer with a contagious laugh; and Liam, a quiet artist with a surprising talent for storytelling around a crackling campfire. The initial awkwardness was palpable, the kind of silent tension that hangs heavy in the air before a first date. But as we started setting up tents, sharing stories about our clumsy attempts at assembling camping gear, the ice began to melt. The shared task – transforming a patch of wilderness into a temporary home – created an immediate sense of unity.

The days were filled with a symphony of natural sounds: the rustling of leaves, the chirping of crickets, the occasional hoot of an owl. We hiked through sun-dappled forests, marveling at the vibrant colors of autumn leaves. We shared stories, laughter, and moments of quiet contemplation, sitting by the campfire, the flames casting dancing shadows on our faces. The conversations weren't always profound; often, they revolved around the mundane aspects of camping—the best way to start a fire, the most effective mosquito repellent, or the funniest mishaps during our hikes. Yet, these everyday exchanges were deeply connective, revealing vulnerabilities and shared experiences in ways that formal settings never could. Jessica shared her anxieties about her upcoming veterinary exams, while Mark revealed a hidden passion for amateur astronomy. Liam captivated us with tales of his childhood adventures, his voice low and resonant under the starry night sky.

One evening, as we were preparing dinner, a sudden downpour turned our campsite into a mud-soaked haven. Instead of despair, laughter filled the air. We scrambled to protect our food, our equipment, and ourselves, helping each other secure tents and belongings. The shared struggle, the camaraderie in facing a sudden challenge, created a bond that words could barely capture. We huddled together inside the largest tent, sharing stories and jokes, the sounds of the rain a soothing rhythm against the background of our laughter. It was in those moments of shared adversity that the true strength of our connection emerged.

The camping trip wasn't just a weekend getaway; it was a transformative experience. It demonstrated the power of shared experiences to forge deep and meaningful bonds, connections built not on superficial pleasantries, but on shared laughter, mutual support, and the quiet understanding that comes from facing challenges together.

Back in the familiar rhythm of everyday life, I

continued to seek out opportunities for shared experiences. I joined a community garden project, working alongside fellow enthusiasts to cultivate a vibrant patch of land. The shared labor, the collective effort in nurturing life from the soil, created a sense of purpose and camaraderie that exceeded my expectations. We shared gardening tips, recipes, and stories about our families, our backgrounds as diverse as the plants we cultivated. The sense of collective achievement, of harvesting the fruits of our labor—literally and metaphorically —forged a deep bond between us.

One particularly memorable day, we were harvesting tomatoes, their skin warm under the summer sun, their aroma rich and intoxicating. As we worked side by side, sharing jokes and stories, a sense of deep connection settled over the group. It wasn't just about the tomatoes; it was about the shared effort, the shared laughter, the shared passion for creating something beautiful together. That sense of shared purpose was a powerful antidote to my old anxieties, a balm to the lingering fear of social interaction.

The community garden wasn't just a patch of land; it was a fertile ground for friendship. The shared experiences of planting, weeding, and harvesting created a sense of belonging, a feeling of being part of something larger than myself. It was a reminder that connection wasn't about forced interactions or contrived conversations; it was about shared purpose, shared effort, and the quiet satisfaction of creating something beautiful together.

I also started volunteering at a local soup kitchen, serving meals to the homeless and less fortunate. The experience was humbling, both personally and socially. The act of serving others, of alleviating suffering, even in a small way, fostered a sense of connection that went far beyond the transactional nature of serving food. The conversations with the people I served were often profound, revealing stories of resilience, perseverance, and the simple human need for connection. It was a stark reminder that despite our differences, our shared humanity transcends all barriers.

The shared experience of volunteering was incredibly fulfilling. The quiet acts of kindness, the small gestures of compassion, built bridges of understanding and connection. It was a reminder that helping others is not only a selfless act; it is also a profoundly social one. The sense of camaraderie among the volunteers was another source of strength and encouragement. We shared stories, challenges, and celebrated small victories together, forging strong bonds through our shared commitment to a common cause.

The Ongoing Journey

My journey wasn't without its setbacks. There were times when anxiety still reared its head, moments when I felt overwhelmed by the prospect of social interaction. But the lessons I'd learned—the power of shared experiences, the importance of active participation, the value of vulnerability—were firmly etched in my mind. I had learned to recognize my anxiety for what it was: a feeling, not a fact. I had learned to manage it, to work through it, to use it as a catalyst for growth.

Nine months after discovering the "Top Secret Guide," my life was profoundly different. The crippling loneliness I had once known was a distant memory, replaced by a vibrant network of friendships and a deep sense of belonging. My journey wasn't about eliminating anxiety; it was about transforming my relationship with it, about using it as a springboard for growth and connection. I had learned that the key to social success wasn't about mastering social skills in isolation; it was about actively seeking opportunities for shared experiences, engaging wholeheartedly in life, and embracing the beauty and challenges of human connection. My newfound confidence wasn't just about social skills; it was about the confidence in my ability to connect authentically with others, to build meaningful relationships, and to create a life rich with purpose and joy. The world was no longer a daunting place; it was an invitation to share experiences, to forge bonds, and to create a life filled with connection and fulfillment. And that, I realized, was the true secret to social success.

The aroma of freshly brewed coffee hung in the air, a comforting scent that mirrored the warmth spreading through my heart. Sunlight streamed through the large windows of the community center, illuminating the faces of my friends gathered around a large, oak table. Jessica, ever the organized one, was meticulously arranging pastries, while Mark, his laughter booming, was engaged in a lively debate with Liam about the merits of different coffee roasts. Sarah, a newcomer to our group whom I'd met at the pottery class, was quietly sketching in her notebook, her brow furrowed in concentration. Around us, the gentle hum of conversation created a symphony of shared laughter and comfortable silences. This wasn't some carefully constructed social event; this was genuine, effortless connection. Nine months ago, this scene would have been unimaginable. Nine months ago, I was a ghost on the periphery, a silent observer rather than an active participant.

This wasn't about some magical transformation. There were no sudden epiphanies, no overnight miracles. It was a gradual, painstaking process, a series of small victories that, when accumulated, had resulted in this incredible shift. The "Top Secret Guide" had been my compass, guiding me through the sometimes-murky waters of social interaction. But the real work had been in the doing, in the consistent application of its principles: mastering my physical energy, asking engaging questions, and actively participating in social events.

I remember the initial trepidation, the overwhelming sense of self-consciousness that accompanied my first tentative steps into the social arena. The fear of rejection, of saying the wrong thing, of being judged—these were my constant companions. But gradually, as I began to practice the techniques outlined in the book, something shifted. My body language became more open and inviting. My voice, once hesitant and subdued, grew stronger and more confident. I started to ask questions, not just to fill the silence, but out of genuine curiosity, a desire to learn about the people around me. I began to listen more than I spoke, truly absorbing what others were sharing, allowing myself to be present in the moment.

The basketball team had been a surprising success. The shared passion for the game, the physical exertion, the camaraderie of teamwork—these had created a natural breeding ground for connection. But it wasn't just about the sport; it was about the shared experiences after the game, the casual conversations, the inside jokes, the genuine interest in each other's lives. I learned to appreciate the power of shared laughter, the ease with which bonds could be formed through simple, everyday moments. The conversations weren't always profound; they often revolved around the mundane—our favorite pizza toppings, our most embarrassing childhood memories, our dreams for the future. But in those mundane exchanges, I discovered the true essence of connection.

The volunteer work at the animal shelter had been a gentle introduction to the power of shared purpose, a chance to contribute to something larger than myself. Caring for the animals, comforting them in their moments of fear, had given me a sense of purpose and fulfillment, but it had also fostered a deep connection with my fellow volunteers. We shared stories about our furry companions, exchanging tips on animal care and celebrating milestones in the animals' journeys. The common goal, the shared compassion for these vulnerable creatures, had created an unbreakable bond between us.

And then there was the camping trip, an adventure that had initially terrified me. The shared challenge of setting up tents, preparing meals, and navigating the wilderness had created an intimacy that words could hardly capture. We had faced a sudden downpour together, laughed through our struggles, and shared stories under the starry night sky. The shared adversity had forged a connection far deeper than any casual encounter.

The community garden had been my most surprising success. I had never considered myself a gardener, yet the act of nurturing life, the shared labor of planting, weeding, and harvesting, had been inexplicably rewarding. The shared purpose, the camaraderie of working together towards a common goal, had fostered an unparalleled sense of belonging. I learned to appreciate the quiet satisfaction of creating something beautiful, the deep sense of accomplishment that came from watching seeds transform into vibrant plants.

The pottery class, on the other hand, had been a reminder that not every social experience would be a resounding success. The initial interactions were stiff, formal, and awkward. I struggled to find common ground with the group, my attempts at conversation falling flat. For the first time since I began my journey, I faced a moment of overwhelming self-doubt. My anxiety reared its head, whispering doubts about my progress.

But this time, I didn't let the setback derail me. I applied the lessons I had learned, choosing to focus on my own contribution, rather than dwelling on the lack of effortless connection. I focused on the joy of creating something with my own hands, finding solace in the rhythm of the potter's wheel. Slowly, cautiously, I began to engage with my fellow students, asking questions about their work, sharing my own experiences, learning from their expertise. And over time, the group warmed to me. The connections were slower to develop, less immediate, but perhaps more rewarding precisely for that reason.

Looking around the table at my friends, I felt a profound sense of gratitude. This wasn't just about having a group of people to spend time with; it was about the quality of those relationships, the genuine connection, the mutual respect and appreciation. It was about belonging, about being seen and accepted for who I was, flaws and all. The loneliness I had once known was a distant memory, a shadowy figure lurking in the recesses of my past.

My journey hadn't been about conquering my anxiety; it had been about learning to live with it, to navigate it, to use it as a catalyst for growth. I had learned that social success wasn't about mastering some set of social skills, but about actively seeking out opportunities for shared experiences, embracing vulnerability, and fostering genuine connections with others.

This wasn't the end of my journey, but a milestone, a testament to the power of consistent effort and self-belief. Maintaining these relationships would require ongoing effort, a continued commitment to active participation, a willingness to be present and vulnerable. There would be challenges, moments of doubt, times when my anxiety might resurface. But I was no longer afraid. I had the tools, the experience, and most importantly, the confidence to navigate those moments, to emerge stronger and more connected than before. My life was no longer defined by loneliness but by a vibrant network of friendships, a testament to the transformative power of shared experiences and the enduring strength of human connection. And that, I realized, was the greatest reward of all.

The journey had changed me, not only socially but profoundly, personally. The quiet, shy man had evolved, empowered by self-belief and bolstered by meaningful connections. And the adventure, I knew, was far from over. The warmth of the coffee, the laughter of my friends, the sunlight streaming through the windows – these were the symbols of a new beginning, a life reborn, vibrant, and deeply connected.

The sun dipped below the horizon, painting the sky in hues of orange and purple as I sat on my porch, a mug of chamomile tea warming my hands. The day had been a whirlwind – a successful presentation at work, a lively dinner with friends, a quiet evening spent reading. Each event, once a source of crippling anxiety, now felt manageable, even enjoyable. The transformation hadn't been magical; it had been a relentless pursuit of self-improvement, a testament to the power of consistent effort and self-belief.

The "Top Secret Guide to Social Success" had provided the initial roadmap, but the true journey lay in the application of its principles, in the countless small victories that accumulated over time. It wasn't about erasing my anxieties; it was about learning to live alongside them, to understand their triggers, and to develop coping mechanisms that allowed me to navigate social situations with greater ease and confidence.

One of the most significant lessons I learned was the importance of self-compassion. There were days when my anxiety overwhelmed me, when the fear of rejection paralyzed me, when I retreated into the safety of solitude. In the past, these setbacks would have been crushing, leading to self-criticism and despair. But now, I treated these moments with the same kindness and understanding I would offer a friend struggling with a similar challenge. I acknowledged my feelings without judgment, recognizing that anxiety was a part of me, not a reflection of my worth.

I also learned the value of setting realistic goals. I didn't expect to become a social butterfly overnight. Instead, I focused on small, achievable steps – attending one social event per week, striking up a conversation with one new person each day, offering a genuine compliment to someone I encountered. Each small success built upon the last, reinforcing my confidence and bolstering my self-belief. The incremental nature of my progress made the overall journey feel less daunting, more sustainable.

This involved identifying my triggers and devising strategies to mitigate their impact. For instance, large crowds used to fill me with overwhelming dread. So, I started by attending smaller gatherings, gradually increasing the size and complexity of the social events I participated in. Over time, my tolerance for crowds increased, and the anxiety associated with them diminished significantly. Similarly, I developed techniques for managing my physical responses to anxiety – deep breathing exercises, progressive muscle relaxation, and mindfulness meditation. These techniques became my silent allies, providing a sense of calm and grounding during moments of stress.

The journey also demanded unwavering self-reflection. After each social interaction, I took time to analyze my experiences, identifying what went well, what could be improved, and what I learned from the encounter. This process of mindful reflection helped me refine my social skills, adapt to different social contexts, and build my confidence over time. It wasn't merely about accumulating social skills; it was about cultivating self-awareness, understanding my strengths and weaknesses, and developing a deeper sense of self-acceptance.

The maintenance of these newly formed connections required consistent effort. It wasn't enough to simply attend social events; I had to actively nurture these relationships, invest time and energy in them, show up consistently, and make an effort to listen attentively and engage meaningfully with my friends. This involved reaching out regularly, making plans, and participating in activities that we all enjoyed. It required a conscious commitment to be present, both physically and emotionally.

It's important to note that setbacks are inevitable. There would be times when my anxiety would resurface, times when social interactions would feel strained, times when I felt overwhelmed and tempted to retreat. But the difference now was that I approached these challenges with a newfound resilience and perspective. I knew that my anxiety didn't define me, that setbacks were a natural part of the journey, and that I had the tools and the experience to navigate them effectively. I viewed setbacks not as failures but as learning opportunities, chances to reflect, adapt, and grow.

The greatest reward of my journey wasn't simply the acquisition of social skills or the formation of friendships. It was the profound transformation in my sense of self-worth and self-acceptance. I learned that my value wasn't contingent on the approval of others, that I was worthy of love and connection regardless of my social skills. The journey had taught me to embrace my vulnerabilities, to celebrate my imperfections, and to find joy in the simple act of being myself.

I discovered the profound power of shared experiences. The camaraderie of teamwork, the shared laughter during a game, the quiet satisfaction of creating something together – these were the things that forged true and lasting connections. The experiences were just as important, if not more, than the outcome. The joy wasn't only in the success but in the journey itself, in the shared laughter, the mutual support, and the sense of community we built together.

This wasn't a destination but an ongoing journey of

self-discovery and growth. The path ahead remains uncertain, but I'm no longer afraid to embrace the unknown. I've learned that the greatest adventures are often the ones we undertake with others, the ones that push us beyond our comfort zones, the ones that challenge us to grow and evolve. The lessons learned aren't just applicable to social situations; they extend to all aspects of life, from work to personal relationships. The core principles – self-awareness, self-compassion, consistent effort – are the cornerstones of a fulfilling and meaningful life.

And so, I encourage you, dear reader, to embark on your own journey toward social confidence. Don't be afraid to take the first step, no matter how small. Embrace your imperfections, celebrate your victories, and learn from your setbacks. Remember that progress is not linear, that setbacks are inevitable, and that your worth is not determined by your social skills. Your journey will be unique, filled with its own challenges and triumphs, but remember the power of consistent effort, self-belief, and the unwavering support of your inner self. The ability to build genuine connections and embrace the beauty of shared experiences is an invaluable gift, one that will enrich your life in ways you can only begin to imagine. Your story, your journey, is waiting to unfold. Take a deep breath, believe in yourself, and begin. The world is waiting to connect with you. People WILL like you! I promise!

Before

After

ACKNOWLEDGME NTS

The "Top Secret Guide…" may not be a real book, but this one is. Freddie has done a great job taking my experiences and words and putting them together in this story.

I want to express my deepest gratitude to my new friends for their unwavering support and encouragement throughout the writing of this book. Their belief in me, even during moments of self-doubt, fueled my perseverance.

Finally, thank you to the countless individuals who shared their stories of overcoming social anxiety. Your courage and vulnerability inspired me and helped us to craft a narrative that resonates with authenticity and hope.

Gary

SUPPLEMENTARY RESOURCES

This appendix provides supplementary resources to help you on your journey toward social confidence:

List of Helpful Organizations: A curated list of organizations that offer support and resources for individuals struggling with social anxiety, including links to their websites.

The Anxiety & Depression Association of America (ADAA) is a national nonprofit organization dedicated to preventing, treating, and coping with anxiety, depression, OCD, PTSD, and co-occurring disorders. Their website offers extensive educational materials, including articles, fact sheets, and webinars, as well as a therapist finder tool to locate mental health professionals specializing in anxiety disorders. https://adaa.org

The National Alliance on Mental Illness (NAMI) is the nation's largest grassroots mental health organization dedicated to building better lives for

the millions of Americans affected by mental illness. NAMI provides advocacy, education, support, and public awareness, offering resources such as local chapters, support groups, and educational programs for individuals and their families. Their website serves as a portal to connect individuals with community-based services and information.
https://www.nami.org

The International OCD Foundation (IOCDF) is a global organization committed to helping individuals affected by obsessive-compulsive disorder (OCD) and related disorders. While the focus is on OCD, many of the strategies and support systems are beneficial for individuals experiencing social anxiety, particularly when social situations trigger intrusive thoughts or compulsive behaviors. They offer resources like expert-led webinars, a directory of OCD specialists, and extensive information on treatment options.
https://iocdf.org

It is vital to seek medical help whenever this may be necessary for physical or mental illness.

If you need to speak with someone who will listen at anytime, ring Samaritans.
https://www.samaritans.org

Sample Conversation Starters: A collection of open-ended questions and conversation prompts to help you initiate and maintain engaging conversations.

Ten such prompts are presented here, designed to facilitate connection and dialogue in various social settings. The intention behind these questions is to move beyond superficial pleasantries and encourage genuine exchange. They are formulated to be adaptable, suitable for initial encounters or for deepening existing relationships. The focus remains on the practical application of these starters in real-world interactions, with the expectation that consistent use will yield positive results in building social confidence and fostering meaningful connections.

The questions are:

"What has been the highlight of your week so far, and why?",

"What's a skill you're currently trying to learn or improve upon?",

"If you could travel anywhere in the world right now, where would you go and what would you do there?",

"What's a book or movie that has recently made a significant impression on you?",

"What's something you're passionate about and would love to share more about?",

"What's a cause or issue that you feel strongly about?",

"What's a piece of advice you've received that has stuck with you?",

"What's a memorable travel experience you've had?",

"What's a simple pleasure that always brings you joy?", and

"What are you looking forward to in the coming days or weeks?".

These questions are structured to invite detailed responses, offering ample opportunity for the other person to elaborate and for follow-up questions to arise organically, thus sustaining the conversation.

The ultimate aim is to equip individuals with practical tools for navigating social interactions more comfortably and effectively. The availability of these resources, from organizational support to specific conversation starters, underscores the structured approach to developing social confidence. The information provided is intended to be actionable, with the understanding that repeated practice and engagement with these resources will contribute to incremental progress in overcoming social anxiety and improving interpersonal skills. The continuity of the journey is emphasized, with the expectation that these supplementary resources are just the beginning of a process of personal growth and development in social confidence.

GLOSSARY

Social Anxiety: A mental health condition characterized by intense fear or anxiety in social situations.

Self-Compassion: Treating oneself with kindness, understanding, and acceptance, especially during difficult times.

Mindfulness: Paying attention to the present moment without judgment.

Progressive Muscle Relaxation: A relaxation technique involving systematically tensing and releasing different muscle groups.

Cognitive Behavioral Therapy (CBT): A type of therapy that helps individuals identify and change negative thought patterns and behaviors.

ABOUT THE AUTHOR

Freddie James

FJ Books for Life by Freddie James are insightful informed guided to issues that we all face in different ways as human beings.

Printed in Dunstable, United Kingdom